D0180082

By STAN KIRBY

Illustrated by GEORGE O'CONNOR

LITTLE SIMON
New York London Toronto Sydney New Delhi

LITTLE SIMON
An imprint of Simon & Schuster Children's Publishing Division • 1230 Avenue of the Americas, New York, New York 10020 • First Little Simon paperback edition October 2014 • LITTLE SIMON is a registered trademark of Simon & Schuster, Inc., and associated colophon is a trademark of Simon & Schuster, Inc. For information about special discounts for bulk purchases, please contact Simon & Schuster Special Sales at 1-866-506-1949 or business@simonandschuster.com. The Simon & Schuster Speakers Bureau can bring authors to your live event. For more information or to book an event contact the Simon & Schuster Speakers Bureau at 1-866-248-3049 or visit our website at www.simonspeakers.com. Designed by Jay Colvin. The text of this book was set in Little Simon Gazette.
Manufactured in the United States of America 0418 MTN 10 9 8 7 6 5 4 3
Library of Congress Cataloging-in-Publication Data
Kirby, Stan. Captain Awesome gets a hole-in-one / by Stan Kirby ; illustrated by George O'Connor. pages cm. — (Captain Awesome ; #12)
Summary: "When Eugene goes mini-golfing for Meredith Mooney's birthday party, he realizes he's actually an excellent mini-golfer! But Meredith realizes this too, and she starts to cheat so that she'll win. Will Eugene reveal her cheating ways?"— Provided by publisher. [1. Superheroes—Fiction. 2. Cheating—Fiction. 3. Miniature golf—Fiction. 4. Birthdays—Fiction. 5. Parties—Fiction.] I. O'Connor, George, illustrator. II. Title. PZ7.K633529Cagk 2014 [Fic]—dc23 2013047670
ISBN 978-1-4814-1432-6 (hc)
ISBN 978-1-4814-1431-9 (pbk)
ISBN 978-1-4814-1433-3 (eBook)

Table of Contents

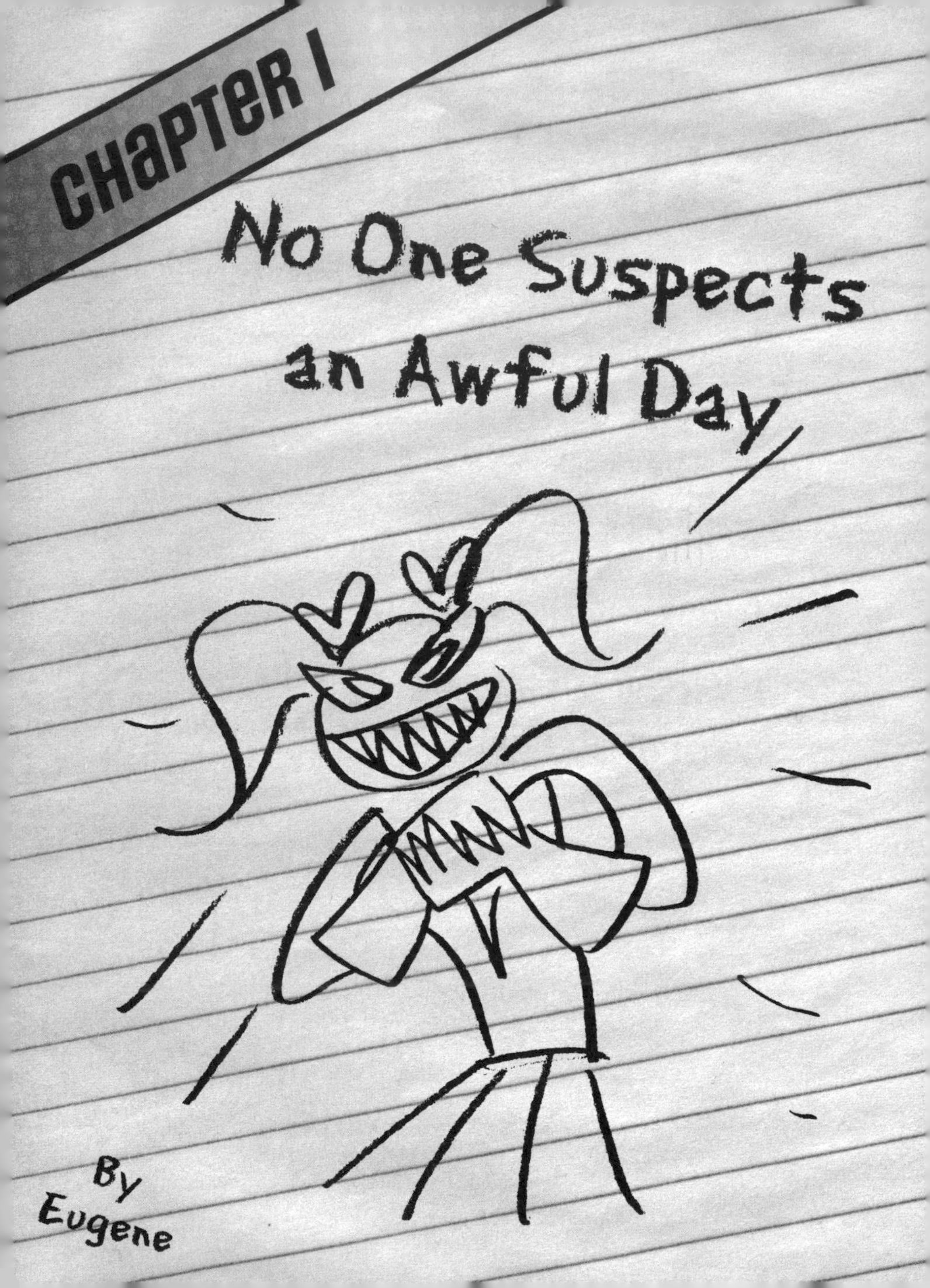
CHAPTER 1
No One Suspects an Awful Day
By Eugene

Today is going to be awesome!"

Those were the words Eugene McGillicudy said when he woke up the morning that all the trouble started.

What he *should* have said but didn't *know* he should have said was:

OH, NO!

It was going to be his worst day ever. But, again, Eugene didn't know that when he woke up.

He didn't even get a hint of his awful day as he walked to Sunnyview Elementary School with his best friends, Charlie Thomas Jones and Sally Williams.

"Smell that fresh air," Eugene said. "This is going to be a great day!"

Charlie nodded. "Let's hurry to class!"

"I do not want to miss one second of a great day," Sally said.

The trio ran all the way to their classroom.

"Morning, Turbo," Eugene said to the class hamster. Turbo looked up from his carrot and squeaked a tiny squeak.

Eugene squeezed his backpack into his cubby and sat at his desk.

His awesome-but-actually-awful day was about to begin.

Eugene's idol, Super Dude, would have sniffed out the evil that was about to strike, but—

Wait, what's that?

You've never heard of Super Dude?

Do you live in a crater on the surface of the dark side of the moon?

How could you not have heard of the greatest superhero in the history of superduperness? Super Dude is the guy who bent back the five fingers of Count Fist-Face and tangled the metal springs of the

bouncy Commander Coil O'Evil.

Super Dude was also the star of the so-real-they-have-to-be-true comic books that made him Eugene's favorite superhero of all time, forever and ever.

Eugene was so inspired by Super Dude's adventures that he created his own alter ego and became Sunnyview's first

superhero . . . CAPTAIN AWESOME!

MI-TEE!

But Eugene wasn't the only superhero in Sunnyview. He was joined by his two best buds, Charlie and Sally. Together, with their class's pet hamster, Turbo, they were:

THE SUNNYVIEW SUPERHERO SQUAD!

SQUAD UP!

Charlie became Nacho Cheese Man—the only hero with the power of canned cheese.

CHEESY YO!

And Sally? She was the superfast Supersonic Sal.

SPEEDY GO!

Together these four heroes put badness in its place. And right now Eugene's baddest badness, Meredith Mooney, was right at the front of the class. Meredith wore so much pink—from her hair ribbons, to her bracelets, to her shoes—that she looked like a strawberry pink milk shake without the cup.

You see, Meredith wasn't just another annoying girly girl. She was secretly the pink villain known as Little Miss Stinky Pinky.

Meredith said to the class, "I have an announcement to make. A big announcement."

"Oh! Oh! Is it about the zombie apocalypse?" Charlie asked. "I love the zombie apocalypse!"

"Or a plague of mutant rats?"

Sally asked. "Should we get our emergency kits ready?"

"I'll bet it's something pink," Eugene said with a sigh. "It's almost *always* about pink."

"As you might know, my birthday is this weekend . . . ," Meredith began.

YAWN.

Charlie elbowed Eugene. "Of course we know," said Charlie. "She circled it on the class calendar."

"And she wrote it on the white-board," whispered Sally.

"And she talked about it *every day* this week," Eugene added.

"Quiet!" Meredith yelled. "My big news is: I'm throwing a huge birthday party! With cake, candy, games, and prizes, and my mom is

making me invite all of you!"

Eugene and Charlie couldn't hear for a minute.

"Are we caught in a whirling space vacuum of the dreaded Planet Suckatron?" Eugene yelled over to Charlie.

But they weren't. The noise was the wild cheers and applause from their classmates.

"Did she just invite us to her party?" Sally asked.

Meredith was still speaking. "We're all going to Max Maxtone's Maxi Mini-Golf!"

A whole day of celebrating MY! ME! MINE! MEREDITH? No!

There's got to be some way out of this horrible horror! thought Eugene as he slumped down in his seat.

Then he perked up. "Saturday is still a few days away. Maybe a comet will smack into the Earth and the party will be canceled!" he said excitedly.

CHAPTER 2
Delivery of Evil!
By Eugene

I think it's very nice that Meredith invited you to her party," Eugene's mom said as they rode the mall escalator.

Charlie and his mom were right behind them because no comet had hit Earth yet.

"But, Mom!" Eugene tried to protest. "It's *Meredith*! Otherwise known as Little Miss Stink—" Eugene stopped himself. He could not give away his secret identity—or the fact that he had a nemesis!

"Your father and I love mini-golf," Eugene's mom replied. "The windmills! The water traps! The colorful golf balls! I wish all sports had a mini version."

"I'd like to see mini-dodgeball," Eugene said.

"I'd like mini-soccer," Charlie said.

WOW!

"Mini-basketball!" Eugene cried.

"Mini-tennis!" Charlie shouted. "Oh, wait. That's Ping-pong."

"So what should we get this nice Meredith for her birthday, Eugene?" Mrs. McGillicudy asked.

"Comic books!" Eugene said. "Or a video game like Deadly Worm Eater 9. Or bagpipes. Yeah, bagpipes!"

Mrs. McGillicudy put her hands on her hips. "I think we'll go to the bookstore," she said.

"And then we can go to the comic book store, right?" Eugene asked.

Eugene's mom nodded as they all walked into Truckload Books, the bookstore that sold books by the truckload.

"I think Meredith would love a new book like this one," said Mrs. McGillicudy. She was holding up a

book from the Critter Club series.

Eugene glanced over. "If it has pink and glitter on it, then it is barftastically perfect," he replied.

MISSION ACCOMPLISHED.

While Eugene's mom paid for the book, Eugene and Charlie

started backing toward the door.

BUT WAIT!

Their exit was blocked. Several large deliverymen were rolling even larger crates through the door. It seemed like there were about 3,462 new truckloads of books being delivered. The way to the comic book store was cut off!

That's when Eugene realized the horrible truth.

These men were not ordinary deliverymen. They were the Blockhead Deliverymen of the wicked Mr. Block-a-Door. Their evil mission was to prevent kids from getting to the places they really wanted to go by blocking their exit doors. Places such as the ice-cream shop, the Build-a-Robot store, and most especially, the comic book store.

This was definitely a job for Captain Awesome!

MI-TEE!

"Stop blocking us, deliverymen!" Captain Awesome commanded.

CHEESY YO!

Nacho Cheese Man pulled out his cans of squirt cheese. "Step aside or you'll get a double blast of Spicy Bacon Ranch!"

The deliverymen didn't move. The way out was still blocked.

Just then Captain Awesome spotted Supersonic Sal rushing to the store.

"Sorry, we're late!" she yelled to the boys. "Mr. Whiskersworth needed his litter box changed."

Then she let out a mighty supersonic scream.

AAAHHHHHHHHHHHH!

The deliverymen let go of their crates and covered their ears. Then Captain Awesome saw his chance. "This way, Nacho Cheese Man!"

The heroes raced from the bookstore,

zigzagging through the legs of the deliverymen. Before the bad guys could recover, Captain Awesome and Nacho Cheese Man were through the door and into the mall!

"Thank you, Supersonic Sal!" Captain Awesome said.

“Don’t thank me,” Supersonic Sal said. “Thank my Supersonic Scream. I’ve been practicing.”

“To the comic book store!” Captain Awesome called out, and charged through the mall with the Sunnyview Superhero Squad . . . and their mothers right behind.

CHAPTER 3
Let the Games Begin!
By
ugene

Welcome to Max Maxtone's Maxi Mini-Golf!" Max Maxtone said at the counter. "Where every hole is a hole-in-one. Sometimes!" He was dressed in baggy green pants, an orange-checkered vest, and a purple hat that looked like a mushroom cap. "Where's the birthday girl?"

"She likes an introduction," Meredith's older sister, Melissa, whispered to Max. "Boys and girls of Sunnyview Elementary," she continued, "it is my duty as older sister to ask for a big welcome for the birthday girl herself: your classmate and Birthday Queen for the day . . . Meredith Mooney!"

Eugene groaned.

"Thank you, everyone, for your birthday wishes and also for the stack of presents on the table." Meredith pointed to a pyramid of gifts wrapped in all shades of pink. "I just know I'm going to love some of them!"

Charlie grabbed a golf club from the rack. "Game on!" He picked an orange ball.

Gil, Neal, Jake, and Ellen grabbed their clubs while Wilma, Howard, Dara, and Olivia got their golf balls first.

"I got teal!" cried Howard.

"Pink!" said Olivia.

"No, no, no!" Meredith walked to the front of the line and took the pink ball from Olivia's hand. "Pink golf balls are only for the

Birthday Queen. You may have blue. Or yellow. Or any other color that's *not* pink."

The kids moved to the first hole. The course had nine holes and a bonus tenth one at the end that offered a once-in-a-lifetime special prize for anyone who got a hole-in-one.

Meredith pushed through the crowd. "As the birthday girl, I'll be going first," she told them. She placed her ball down.

"Everyone, stand back while I warm up," she commanded. She adjusted her pink bracelets, retied the pink ribbon in her hair, and tapped her right foot—and pink shoe—on the ground. "Let glitter be my guide!"

Meredith gave the ball a solid whack. It flew over the first bump on the green, raced up and over the second, ricocheted off a brick wall, rolled back over both bumps, and landed at her feet. She stomped her foot. "Pink has never let me down before!" she said. Then she hit the ball again.

SMACK!

On the seventh try, Meredith finally got the ball in the hole.

"She's not very good at this, is she?" Charlie whispered to Sally.

The rest of the class didn't do very well either. Gil's ball never made it up the first hill. Dara whiffed

every time. Charlie was nervous and overshot the hole . . . though his ball did go into hole number seven!

And then it was Eugene's turn.

"Let the superstrength of Super Dude guide my mighty aim," said Eugene.

Eugene lined up his club with his ball and took a practice swing.

He cleared his throat, shook his right leg like he was trying to free a

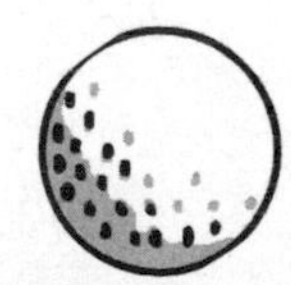

mouse from his pants, took a deep breath, and—

"Ugh. Would you hurry up?" Meredith complained.

"Mini-golf is a game of skill," Eugene said. "I'm almost done with my skilling."

SWING! Eugene smacked the ball. It shot like a rocket over the first bump, jumped over the second bump, and rolled just inches from the hole.

"Yes!" Eugene said. He ran to the hole and, with a second shot, knocked the ball in. "A hole-in-two!"

"Whatever." Meredith crossed her arms, and the group headed to the second hole.

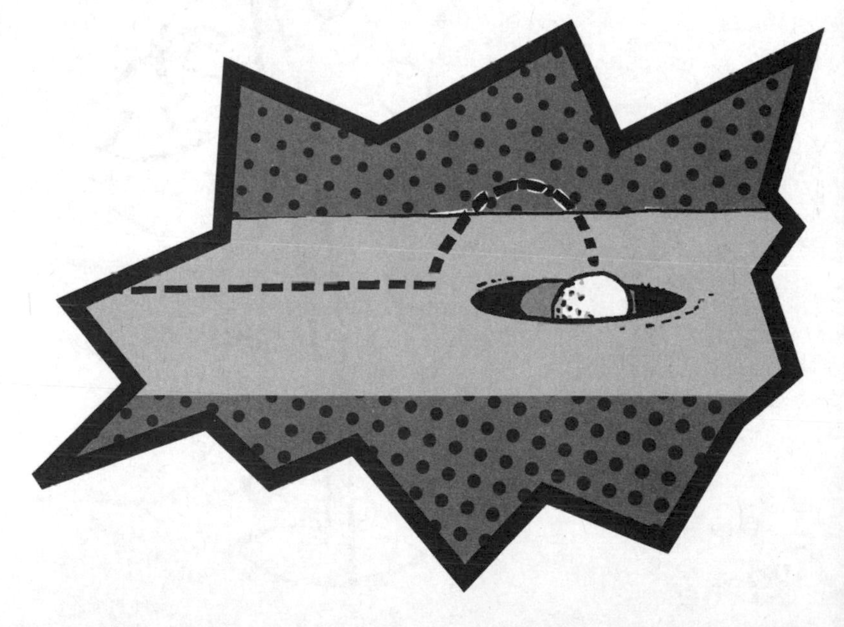

CHAPTER 4

A Hole in Six . . . or Seven . . . or Eight

2

By Eugene

The second hole was just a little harder. The ball had to turn a corner and go up a ramp to make it into the hole.

Charlie went first. He smacked his orange ball down the golf green. It almost got up the ramp, but then it stopped and rolled back to him.

It took six more shots before Charlie got it right.

"My turn!" Eugene said. "May

the superstrength of Super Dude guide my ball again!" He hit his ball. It stopped just inches from the hole. He gently tapped it in. Another hole-in-two.

Meredith rolled her eyes. Then she swung her club.

WHIFF!

She missed.

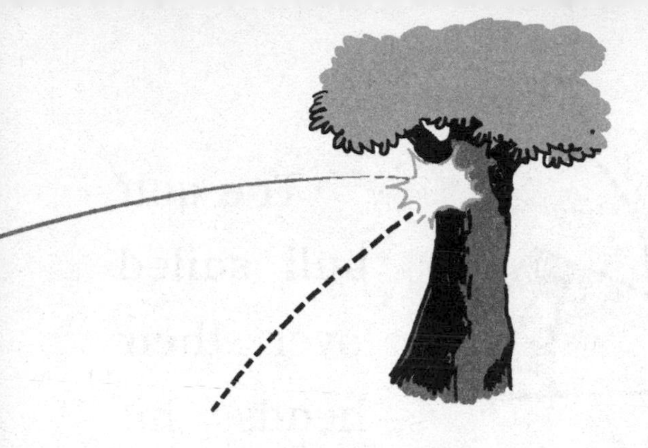

"Strike one," Eugene said.

"No, strike zero," Meredith corrected. "Birthday girls get a free swing."

She leveled her club again and took aim. She raised her club slowly . . . and swung! The ball flew into the air and bounced off a tree.

"Incoming!" Sally called out. The kids dropped to the ground.

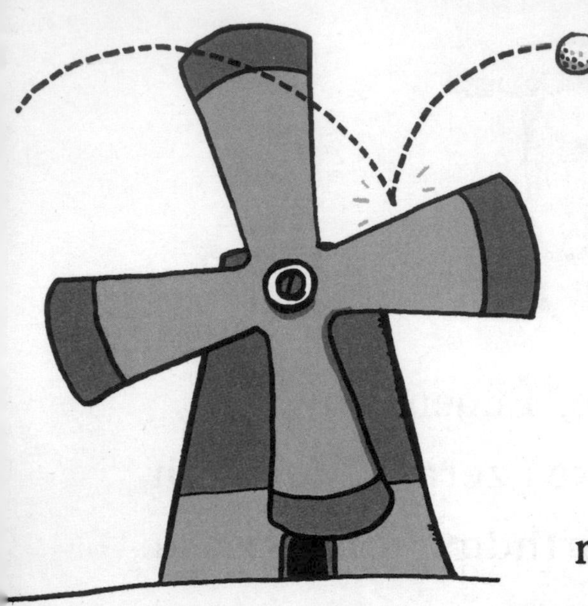

The golf ball sailed over their heads, hit the blades of the wind-mill on hole number nine, spun back, and landed only a foot from hole number two.

"I meant to do that," Meredith said with a smile.

But it still took her four more tries to get the ball into the hole.

"Argh! Stupid golf club!" Meredith

stormed back to exchange her club for a new one.

By the third hole, Meredith had discovered the secret to mini-golf. "All your googly eyes are throwing off my game," she insisted. "From now on, no one can watch me."

Meredith went last while everyone moved on to the fourth hole. And she did better. "I got a three!" she announced when she caught up to the group. "I knew it was your fault," she told Eugene.

Meredith got a hole-in-one on the fifth hole, putting her in second

place. Right behind Eugene.

"Go help yourselves to juice and cake," Meredith said. "I won't be long. This hole looks pretty easy for a mini-golfer as good as I am."

CAKE?!

That was all anyone needed to hear. The kids ran to the party

area where Meredith's mom and Melissa had set up a table packed with birthday treasures: cake, ice cream, chocolate, juice, and all the wonderful junk food kids joyfully stuff themselves with at birthday parties.

As everyone squished and squeezed around the table, Eugene

peered back toward the sixth hole to see if Meredith was coming. There was only one word to describe what Eugene saw next . . .

SHOCK!

Meredith picked up her ball and dropped it into the hole. "I got another two!" she yelled, not realizing Eugene was watching her. "I'm in first place!"

Eugene gasped. No wonder Meredith was getting better at mini-golf.

She was cheating!

CHAPTER 5
No Barfy Cake for You
By Eugene

"Happy birthday to you! Happy birthday to—" the students from Ms. Beasley's second-grade class began to sing as Melissa carried in the birthday cake. But they were promptly interrupted by Meredith's hands waving urgently.

"Stop! Stop! Stop the singing!" Meredith called out. "That junky old song might be good enough for *your* lame birthdays, but I wrote my

own version for you to sing."

Meredith handed out sheets of new lyrics to everyone.

Eugene looked at the lyric sheet and began to read. "Happy birthday to you! No one's more awesome than you! You're the greatest mini-golfer in the whole world. . . . Happy birthday to you!" he read in disbelief. "Meredith expects us to sing this?!" he asked Charlie.

"Well *I'm* not going to sing it," Charlie said.

"No sing song, no eat cake," Meredith replied, leaning in to the boys' conversation.

Hearing Meredith's reply, the rest of the class immediately began to sing. "Happy birthday to you! No one's more awesome than you!"

While the kids enjoyed some cake, Meredith opened her presents. She tore at the wrapping paper like a rabid samurai cat attacking a tissue box with its claws. She rattled off quick replies to each gift as she tossed them back over her shoulder.

"Already have it. Don't want it. As if. Ewww. Where's the receipt? Ummmm . . . whatever. Whoever said, 'It's the thought that counts,' never got *this* as a present."

And with that, Meredith tossed the last gift atop the pile of

presents. She pulled out the mini-golf scorecard. "All right, now let's see how badly I'm beating everyone at mini-golf," she said. "What a surprise! I'm tied with Eu-germ for first place!" Meredith stuck her tongue out at Eugene.

MINI GOLF

HOLE	PAR	Meredith	Eugerm	Stan	Sally
1	2	7	2	4	5
2	3	5	2	6	7
3	2	3	4	5	10
4	3	3	4	7	3
5	4	1	5	10	3
6	2	2	4	4	4
TOTAL	19	21	21	36	32

"What place am I in?" Charlie asked.

"You're so far behind the rest of us that we had to get a second

scorecard just for you." Meredith held up another scorecard that had Charlie's name written in last place.

Charlie sighed. "I thought birth-days were supposed to be fun."

"They are," Eugene assured him. "Unless you're evil." He glared at Meredith.

CHAPTER 6

Beware of Abraham Lincoln!

By Eugene

With their stomachs full of cake, ice cream, gummy candy, and other sugar-coated deliciousness, the kids gathered at the next hole, also known as Mount Crushmore.

George Washington. Thomas Jefferson. Theodore Roosevelt. Abraham Lincoln. Four of the great Presidents of the United States appeared on Mount Rushmore . . . and now here they were on a mini-golf course obstacle.

"Why do they call this hole 'Mount Crushmore'?" Eugene asked.

"Because if you hit your ball into Lincoln's mouth, he crushes it with his teeth," Charlie explained. "I came here last month with my mom and dad, and Honest Abe ate four of my golf balls before I managed to get one past him."

"The trick is to try to aim for Washington's mouth," Sally explained. "That'll put your golf ball right next to the hole when it lands on the other side."

"This time, whoever is in last place goes first," Meredith called out. "Now, who was that again? Hmmmmmmmmm. Wasn't it *you*, Charlie?" She gave him an evil smile.

Charlie dropped his ball down on the green. "We meet again, Abe Lincoln," Charlie murmured,

squinting his eyes like a cowboy in a Western showdown.

"You can do this, Charlie," Eugene encouraged him. "It's just like the time in Super Dude No. 55."

Charlie gave a determined thumbs-up, knowing exactly what Eugene was talking about. He swung his club, smacked the ball, and watched it fly right into Abraham Lincoln's mouth.

Gnarr! Gnarr! Gnarr!

The horrible sound filled Charlie's ears as the sixteenth president of the United States crunched his golf ball.

"NOOOOOOOOOOOOOOOO!" Charlie fell to his knees. "You may be one of America's greatest presidents, but you're pure evil to me!"

"Congratulations, Charlie. If it's possible to do even worse than last place, you just did it." Meredith smiled.

One by one, the remaining kids each took their turn trying to hit their golf ball into George Washington's

mouth. But no one could.

Abraham Lincoln destroyed the golf balls of Jake, Olivia, and Stan. The remaining kids played it safe and hit their golf balls into Roosevelt's and Jefferson's mouths. The golf balls rolled down the tunnels behind the presidents' heads and ended up far from the hole.

Then it was Eugene's turn. He placed his ball on the putting green, carefully swung back his club, and . . . *SMACK*! The blue golf ball rolled right into George Washington's mouth!

"I cannot tell a lie!" a robotic voice announced from a speaker in George Washington's head. "Nice shot!"

Eugene, Charlie, Sally, and the rest of the kids ran to the other side of the presidents and waited for Eugene's ball to come out of the small tunnel. It seemed like a billion years before the ball trickled out, slowly rolled toward the hole, and stopped just at the edge. Eugene took his club and gently tapped the

ball into the hole. He had scored a two on one of the hardest mini-golf holes on the course!

MI-TEE!

But Eugene's moment of victory was cut short when he turned and saw Meredith use her hand to

roll her own golf ball into George Washington's mouth.

"Did you see that?" Eugene whispered to Sally and Charlie. "Meredith just cheated *again*!"

"I cannot tell a lie! Nice shot!" George Washington's robotic voice announced again.

The kids quickly backed away from the hole as Meredith's ball popped out from the tunnel, rolled across the green, and fell into the hole.

"Wow! Another hole-in-one for Meredith!" Jake called out.

Meredith walked over and plucked out her golf ball as the

other kids cheered her on. None of them had seen what Eugene saw.

"Looks like you're in second place, Lose-Gene," Meredith said to Eugene with an evil smile.

CHAPTER 7
The Windmill
of Doom
By
Eugene

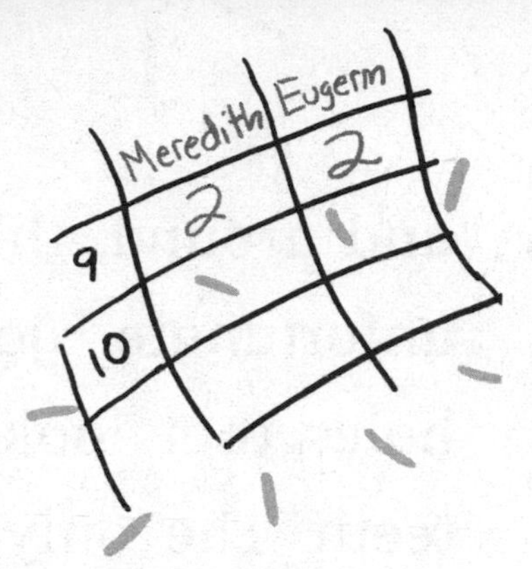

By the time they reached the ninth hole, Eugene and Meredith were tied for first again. And things did not get any easier.

The ninth hole had a large windmill that sat between the golf tee and the hole. The Raging River of No Return surrounded the hole and raged, waiting to take away anyone's ball. The windmill's four blades of doom circled around and around, threatening to knock unfortunate golf balls into two holes that looked like caves with teeth. The only way through was

a path directly under the windmill and past the twirling blades.

When it was Charlie's turn, he studied the whirling windmill blades, waiting for the perfect moment. He waited . . . and waited . . . and—

"NOW!" Eugene cried, eager to help out his best friend.

Charlie smacked his ball. It zoomed toward the dreaded windmill, and just when it looked like it was in the clear, a windmill blade smacked the ball into one of the cave holes.

"Ughhhh!" Charlie cried. "Next birthday party, I want to go bowling!"

"Nice hit, *Chuck*. Now watch how a mini-golf pro does it." Meredith nudged Charlie to the side and put down her ball. But instead of hitting it, she suddenly pointed behind everyone. "Look!" She gasped. "Abe Lincoln just ate a golfer!"

Everyone turned to look. Meredith quickly grabbed her ball and rolled it toward the windmill blades.

"Abe Lincoln didn't eat anyone," Eugene said when he turned around, slightly disappointed. "What are you talking about?"

But then he saw Meredith's ball rolling toward the windmill. *It was all a distraction so Meredith could cheat again!* he realized.

But this time, even cheating didn't help.

SMACK!

SPLASH!

A windmill blade hit Meredith's golf ball. It flew into the air and landed in the Raging River of No Return.

Charlie gasped. "If the ball goes over the Wild, Wild Waterfall, Meredith is out of the game!" he told Eugene and Sally. “That’s part of the rules!”

CHAPTER 8

Captain Awesome Joins the Game

By Eugene

Maybe we should just watch!" Sally said.

"I've always wanted to see a ball go over the waterfall," Charlie added.

Eugene thought for a moment. Then he sighed. "Guys, not even Meredith deserves that," he told his friends. "*Especially* on her birthday."

"Then there's only one thing we can do," Sally replied.

BACKPACKS!
UNZIP!
CAPE!
SUPERHEROES!

Captain Awesome, Nacho Cheese Man, and Supersonic Sal burst onto the scene. They were

ready to save all golf balls that needed saving.

"Everyone, stand back! This is a job for the Sunnyview Superhero Squad!" Captain Awesome cried.

"Save my golf baaaaaaall!" Meredith screeched. "It's the only pink one I haaaaaaaaaaaaaave!"

Supersonic Sal dashed ahead of Captain Awesome and Nacho Cheese Man. She dropped to her

knees at the water's edge and strained to grab the ball.

"I . . . can't . . . reach . . . it . . . it's . . . too . . . far," she said as the current carried the ball toward the waterfall.

"Let my canned cheese do the work!" Nacho Cheese Man held up his canned cheese. He raced ahead of the ball and pressed the button on the can.

A stream of cheddar shot out and covered the rocks that sat in the water just before the waterfall. And just in time! Meredith's golf ball bonked off one rock, then another, and then it stuck to the cheese on the very last rock at the top of the Wild, Wild Waterfall!

“We did it!” Supersonic Sal cheered.

“Yeah, but how are we going to get the ball out of the Raging River of No Return?” Nacho Cheese Man asked. “I don’t think it’s safe for one of us to go into the water.”

What would Super Dude do? Eugene thought so hard, his head hurt. Then he remembered Super Dude No. 199.

"Guys! Do you remember when Super Dude used his cape to catch the nuclear egg grenade thrown by Eggs Benedict Arnold so it wouldn't hit the ground and explode? Watch this!"

Captain Awesome took off his cape. He held the ends and spun the middle around until the cape looked like a long, thick rope. He aimed at the golf ball and . . .

CRACK!

Captain Awesome used his cape to whip the golf ball from the water! The ball bounced off the side of the river and over a grass slope, rolled around the edges of the ninth hole . . . and dropped in!

GASP! Everyone gasped. Meredith looked at the Superhero Squad and smiled. "I hope everyone saw what just happened. I got a hole-in-one!"

Everyone went to congratulate Meredith. Then they moved on to the next hole.

Eugene stuffed his Captain Awesome cape into his bag. He hung back to talk to Meredith. "I know you're cheating," he said to her.

"What?! Who?! Me?! NEVER!" Meredith cried. "I don't know what superpowers you have, Captain Lame-O, but super*sight* obviously isn't one of them."

"Have you ever read Super Dude number 244?" Eugene asked.

"You're joking, right?" Meredith replied.

"Tic-Tac-Terrible was cheating at Galactic Space Checkers. Every time he cheated, Super Dude caught him," Eugene said. "But Tic-Tac-Terrible kept cheating because he

wanted to win so badly. In the end he was working so hard at cheating that he forgot to have any fun. And do you know what Super Dude said?"

"Ummmm . . . don't play checkers with Tic-Tac-Tofu?" Meredith asked.

"Tic-Tac-*Terrible*, and no, Super Dude said, 'Winning isn't everything and cheating spoils the fun for everyone,'" Eugene explained. "Especially the cheater."

Meredith crossed her arms and glared angrily at Eugene. "Whatever, Eugene," she said.

At the same time, both Meredith and Eugene realized that she had called him by his real name. Suddenly they couldn't help but smile. Then Meredith turned and walked to the tenth hole.

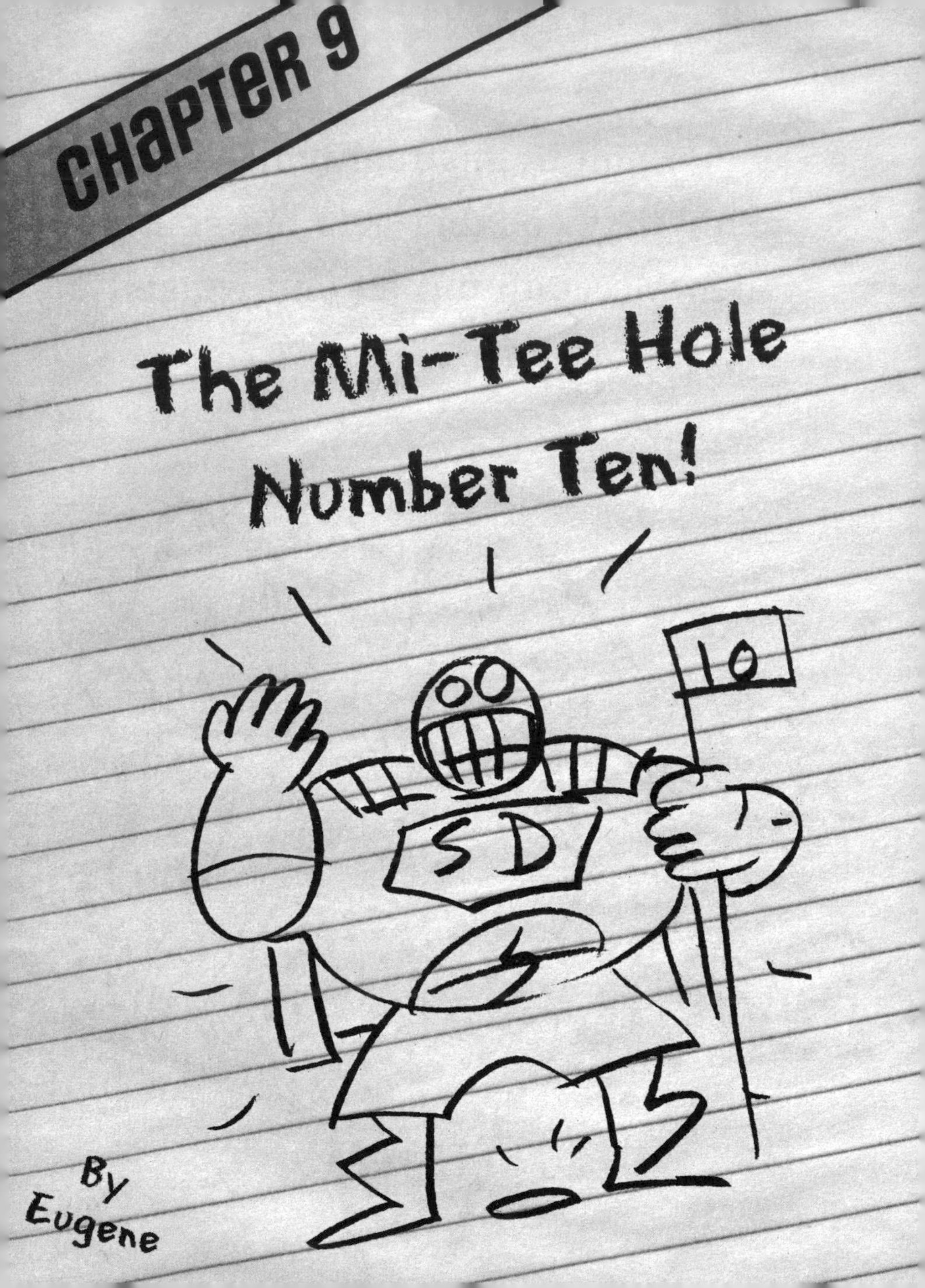
CHAPTER 9
The Mi-Tee Hole
Number Ten!
10
SD
By
Eugene

The kids gathered at the special tenth and final hole. Not *only* was it the last hole, and not *only* would any kid lucky enough to score a hole-in-one get a surprise, but standing over the hole itself was Super Dude!

Or at least a big plastic statue of Super Dude.

“Whoaaaa,” Eugene, Charlie, and Sally said at the same time.

Each partygoer placed their golf balls down, and each partygoer missed. But they didn't really care. They were all eager to see how the Mini-Golf-Battle-of-the-Century between Eugene and Meredith would end.

All Eugene had to do was hit his ball past the supervillain obstacles in fewer strokes than Meredith and he'd be the winner.

"By all that's MI-TEE, let Super Dude guide my ball!" Eugene cried. He took a deep breath. Then he whacked his golf ball.

The ball ricocheted right off Doctorpus and his eight arms of chaos! It bounced past the League of Evil Babysitters! It spun past the vacuum pull of the villainous El-Sucko! It went up a small hill, rolled down the other side, smacked into the heroic feet of Super Dude . . . and rested right

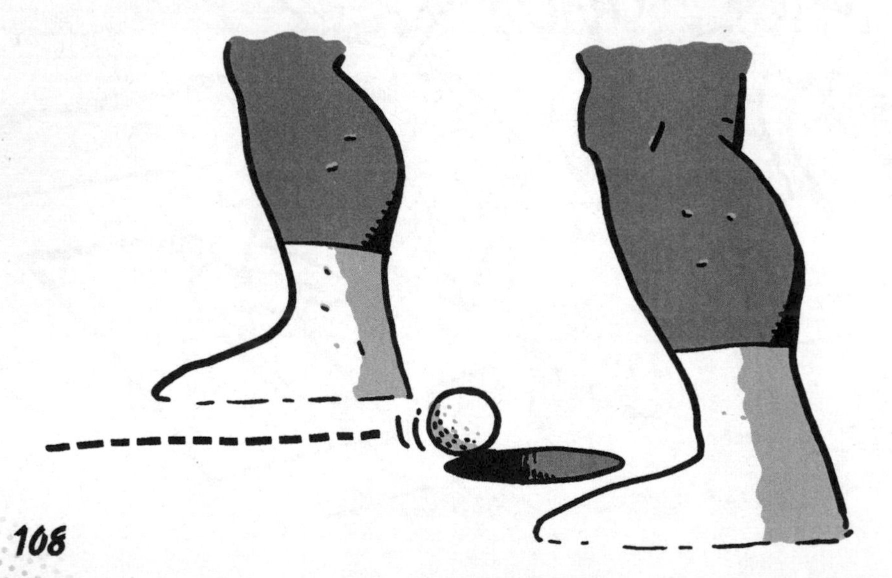

on the edge of the hole. Eugene tapped in the ball with his golf club.

"MI-TEE!" Eugene shouted. "Thank you, heroic feet of Super Dude!"

The only way Meredith could beat him now was if she got a hole-in-one.

The kids turned to Meredith.

Meredith stood, with her golf ball in hand, and looked up at the

towering plastic Super Dude statue. She stood motionless for what seemed like an eternity, then she sighed and dropped her ball onto the ground.

Eugene waited for her to tell everyone to look away. But she never did.

Meredith gripped the club in her hands. She gave the ball a steady whack. It shot past the supervillain obstacles, bounced off Super Dude's left foot, and fell into the hole.

"I got a hole-in-one!" Meredith jumped up and down and cheered louder than she had all day. "Yes! Thank you, Super Dude!"

Everyone cheered for the birthday girl.

Eugene didn't even care that he had lost to Meredith. It was an awesome shot, and she had played the last hole fair and square.

"No one *ever* gets a hole in one on that hole!" Max Maxtone cried. "We have two prizes for the winner and runner-up. The winner gets to choose which one they want," he said as he held out two wrapped packages.

Meredith closed her eyes, took a deep breath, and said, "The one on the right!"

Max handed her the prize and she ripped off the paper.

"Ugh! What's this?!" Meredith growled, holding up a superduper-size stuffed doll.

"Why, that's Tic-Tac-Terrible!" Max Maxtone explained. "He's a Super Dude villain. See, one time he was playing checkers against Super Dude and—"

"What?!" Eugene interrupted Max Maxtone as he opened up his

prize: It was a pair of fuzzy pink bedroom slippers.

"Those are for your feet," Max said proudly. "To keep them cozy and warm."

Meredith and Eugene looked at each other and then down at their prizes.

Faster than anyone could say, "Switcheroo," Eugene and Meredith traded prizes.

Eugene smiled to himself. It had been a day of ups and downs, but he knew he had taught Meredith an important lesson. *And* he had come in second place!

THE

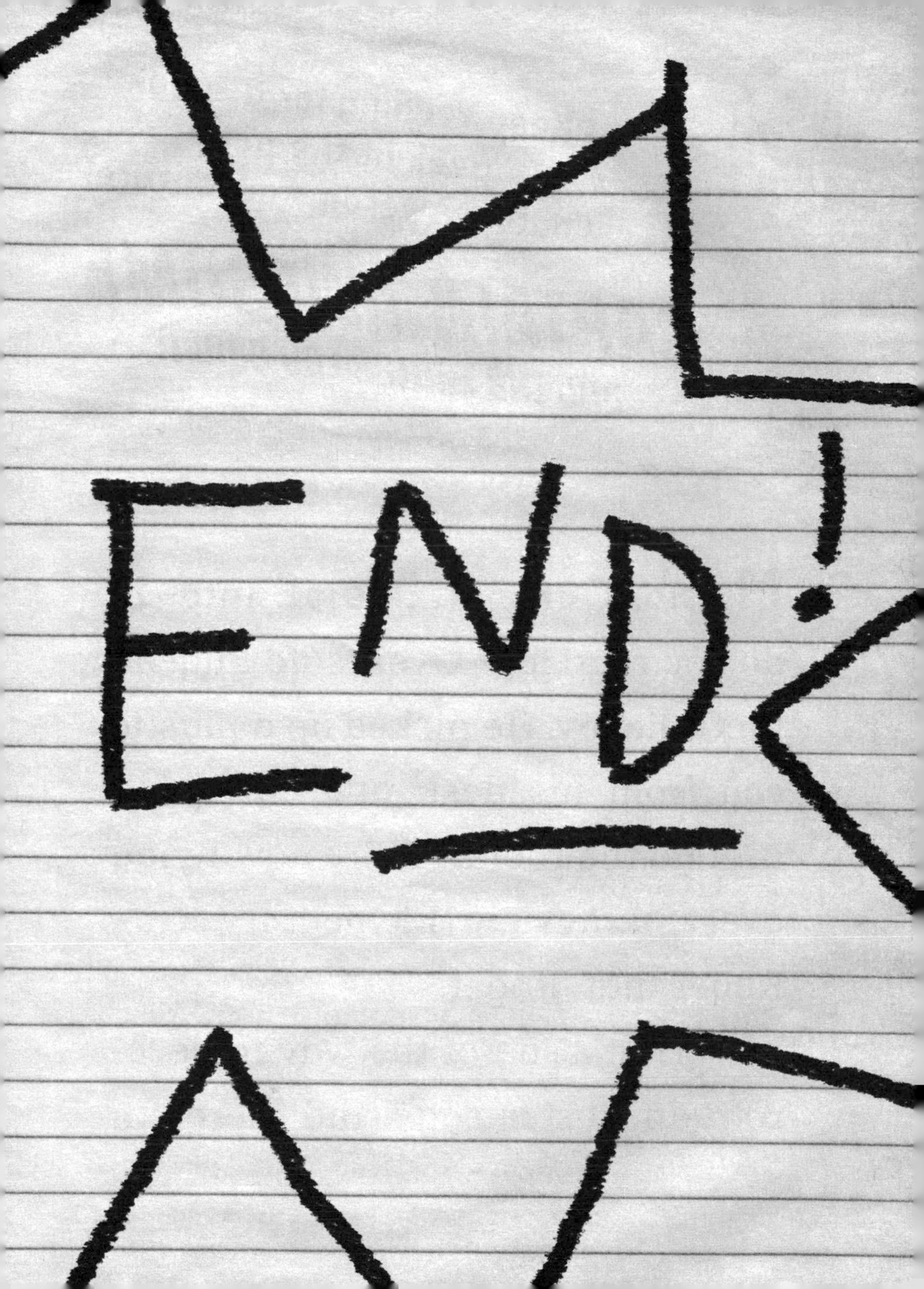
END!

"Mission Control, this is Eggle-1, do you read me? Over," said Eugene McGillicudy. He picked up a plastic egg from his desk and carried it around the room. "We're now flying over Sunnyview Elementary. . . . Roger that, Roger."

"That's so not the way to decorate an Easter egg," said Meredith

Mooney, the pinkest girl in school. She was dressed in a pink skirt that matched the pink bow in her hair. Her light pink shirt matched her light pink shoes that blinked with pink lights on the toes. "What's that supposed to be, anyway?" she asked.

"If you must know—My! Me! Mine! Mere-DITH! It's Eggle-1," Eugene said. "It carries egg-stronauts to the twelve slots on the orbiting Space Carton."

"Oh, good grief," Meredith said with a groan.

CAPTAIN AWESOME FANS:
MEET
ZACK!
His new book series
is out of this world!
GALAXY ZACK
HELLO, NEBULON!
GALAXY ZACK
JOURNEY TO JUNO
GALAXY ZACK
THE PREHISTORIC PLANET
GALAXY ZACK
MONSTERS IN SPACE!
#4
GALAXY ZACK
THREE'S A CROWD!
#5
GALAXY ZACK
A GREEN CHRISTMAS!
#6
GALAXY ZACK
A GALACTIC EASTER!
#7
Visit
GalaxyZackBooks.com
for intergalactic
activities, chapter
excerpts, and the
series' trailer!
Little Simon